I0760679

Praise for

La Bruja in the Orchard

La Bruja in the Orchard is a fast but highly entertaining read. Señora Estrada drew me into the world of 5-year-old Mona, the little girl who sees what goes on around her without understanding some of it. Where did her brother Pancho go and why is her sister Christi so mean to her? She longs to escape her hurtful home, and in the end she finds escape in a way that I wasn't expecting.

Estrada writes like I do, using our Spanish words for effect, reminding us of our own pasts because of what her characters go through, making us see the cruelty in some people and the justice they get at the hands of those who fight back. I highly recommend this book to those of you who like my own books.

-Carmen Baca, *Bella, Collector of Cuentos*

Equal parts *The House on Mango Street* and Mexican folklore, this story is a chilling modern-day fable told through the eyes of Chicano children trying to navigate the terrors that haunt them.

-Pedro Iniguez, *Synthetic Dawns and Crimson Dusks*

When it comes to Latin American Literature, you cannot go wrong with *La Bruja in the Orchard*. The story lays true to Mexican-American mythology, while keeping the reader mystified throughout by allowing them to relate to lead character.

-P.A. O'Neil, *Two Sides of the Same Coin*

Little Mona is the big, big star of this instantly immersive tale of family pain, love, terror, and power. You are immediately dropped into the tone and rhythm of a household and its lives that many know too well, love too much to leave, and know too much to stay in, but do, sometimes in ways they wish they hadn't. This book is gonna get you. You'll see.

-Theodore C. Van Alst, *Pour One for the Devil: A Gothic Novella*

La Bruja in the Orchard is a captivating story that does what many of my favorite stories do, which is to take folklore and imbue it with fresh perspective and emotional depth. It's a haunting tale saturated with a mythical, dreamlike quality. Dr. Estrada takes the reader into a child's world, a scary environment where reality and imagination intersect, and where the complexities of family relationships build toward a climax both painful and cathartic.

-Aleco Julius, *Endless Depths*

La Bruja in the Orchard

María J. Estrada

BARRIO BLUES PRESS
Chicago 2024

For Aaron, the best husband and supporter anyone could ask for! ¡Te Adoro!

FIRST EDITION, APRIL 2024
LA BRUJA IN THE ORCHARD

La Bruja in the Orchard
Barrio Blues Press
Chicago, IL 60609
Barriobluespress.com
(312) 685-1602
Hardcover: I.S.B.N.-978-1-954444-07-2

THIS IS A WORK OF FICTION. Any similarities to dialogue, people, places, and events are purely coincidental and the work of the author's hyperactive, barrio imagination. Any similarities to events or individuals, living or dead, of any vatos or chavas, are entirely coincidental y puros cuentos.

First paperback edition, self-published, 2018.

Printed in the United States of America

"Sometimes I wonder if it's us regular people who unintentionally imbue something with power because we want to be scared of it, we want to explain away the disturbing images we register as being due to some otherworldly evil."

-Cynthia Pelayo, The Shoemaker's Magician (Chicago Saga Book 2)

La Bruja in the Orchard

LITTLE MONA MISSED HER BROTHER, PANCHO, with all of her five-year-old heart. She sat on the prickly orange sofa wearing large white slippers he bought for her. The side where he usually sat was dented and alone. She couldn't quite bring herself to put any of her stuffed animals there, and no one was allowed to sit in his spot. Last week when her stupid sister Christi sat there, Mona had started screaming until she turned light green and threw up all over the place. Her sister jumped up, crying to her mother for help. Later, Christi exacted her revenge by pinching a trail of bruises on Mona's arms.

Now, Mona tried to persuade her Mami and Papa. "Why can't I come?" she asked with her best pleading voice, making her lower lip quiver on command.

"That is no place for little girls," her indignant father had said. "There are murderers and rapists—" Before she asked what a rapist was, her father stopped, giving his mother "the look" and walked out the front door. Mona had been admiring his Sunday best, his black pants, a tender blue guayabera, embroidered with wheat stalks and small boulders. It was the fancy shirt he wore to weddings, but there was nothing of the anticipation of going to a party that Thursday afternoon. No Old Spice cologne, the smell she loved. He looked handsome like

Jorge Negrete, the movie icon his Mami swooned over. Jorge had the moustache all men envied, perfectly groomed and even. Like Jorge, her father walked head high like he was someone important with his hair combed like a T.V. star to the side. His flawless black moustache was also the envy of her older brother.

Her mother, on the other hand, always looked uncomfortable in her party dresses and shoes, just like Mona did in her ruffled dresses and stiff buckled shoes. Often, her mother would slouch which her father would correct by hitting her between her shoulder blades, so she could be worthy of standing next to him. That afternoon, Mami wore her yellow K-mart dress with short sleeves and a curved neckline, dotted with miniscule satin flowers. The matching shoes were the only high heels she used, which according to her mother were baby heels. She complained the shoes were overly snug and caused blisters no matter how many times she stuffed them with newspaper. The dress had been on sale and was tight in the middle and arms. Today, her glossy brown hair was in a long plait with a thick golden ribbon at the end. It almost reached her waist, and her sister habitually said Mami styled it like old ladies from the ranchito, where men still rode horses, and women only donned dark uncool skirts. Her parents weren't stylish and Americanos, nowhere close to Christi's flair. Still, for Mona, her Mami was an elegant princess, right out of a Disney cartoon. Mona knew they weren't going to a party, but she would have given away her Barbie, Kathy, to get dressed up and go.

Her mother smiled weakly, the dark circles under her eyes, accentuating her sadness, "We will be back tomorrow, Little Chick. The place where your brother is at is far away, a four-hour drive to that awful place in Phoenix, the new Alhambra Center; it's a place for people who are being punished. We have to see him early in the morning because he may have to go somewhere new in California, depending on that pinche judge. Plus, amorcito, they don't allow beautiful princesses like you there."

Sucking in her stomach, she crouched awkwardly, put her finger under Mona's chin, and looked straight into her eyes, "Besides, who will take care of the new baby goats and little chicks? Your sister doesn't know how to feed them, and she'll forget to give them water. They'll die in this heat." She waited until Mona nodded, her lower lip trembling in a final plea. Then, Mami gave her a powerful hug and turned to Christi to give final instructions. Christi got no hug.

Today, her annoying sister wore pink rollers in her hair and an inappropriate nighty. It was a see-through light blue that accentuated her budding breasts. She claimed she was hot because of the humid weather, but it was always humid in the orange groves of Somerton, Arizona, and none of the older fourteen-year-old girls

Mona knew dressed like *that*. Christi gave her mother a confident smile, "Don't worry, Ma. She'll be fine. Besides, Mona's a big girl. She's going to kindergarten next fall and can practically take care of herself." Christi stood tall and arrogant because in the past few weeks she had grown taller than her mother, something her sister pointed out all the time.

Her mother gave her an exasperated look, "*Christina Luz Constancia*, I want you two to get along. Warm her milk. Oh, and Mrs. Rodriguez next door, she'll come the moment you call. Poor viejita hasn't slept since her husband died three months ago." She crossed herself, "You call her. Por cualquier cosa. Hear me?"

SMART PANCHO ONCE EXPLAINED to Mona that they lived outside the city limits in the middle of the orange groves. He made her memorize the address, 1426 Avenue B, and important landmarks, such as the nearby nursery. She knew the old wooden house where they lived belonged to the C.C. Howard Company where her father worked, and he was to maintain the orange trees and property. He told this to her, in case she ever got lost. An acre away, they had one neighbor, Mrs. Rodriguez, a kind old woman who made everything from scratch, even goat cheese.

Mona loved visiting her, and a few months ago, had taken it upon her tiny self to take the old woman some sweet rolls. That led to a real beating with a belt from Papa. Christi had been babysitting her and never realized Mona left the house.

"YEAH, YEAH," SAID CHRISTI heading to the sofa and sitting in *his* spot.

As soon as Mami left, Christi turned to Mona and looked up from her T.V. show, "You're going to bed as soon as I'm done feeding you, and don't come out unless you have to pee, or else! But first, take the broom and sweep all the floors." This was the sister Mona knew, the one who would sit on her and pound her arms until they turned purple. The sister who would pinch her when her mother wasn't looking. Christi was cruel, unless her parents or brother were around, but Pancho wasn't home anymore.

He was a senior in high school and about to graduate. Christi was a freshman and despite her nature, he always protected her. Mona couldn't understand why he stood up for her, even the time Mona went to Mrs. Rodriguez's house, Pancho blamed himself for not latching the front door when he went out with friends. Never Christi.

Five months ago, the previous time he got in serious trouble defending *her*, he had gotten into a fight with four cholos, members of the West Side gang, when one of them said, "Bring that fine culo over here, and sit on my face." His sneer and slicked black hair had provoked a smile from Christi, but Pancho would have none of it. Mona overheard her parents talking about what that nasty boy said, and her mother had commented on how Christi needed to be more modest in her dress. Mona thought sitting on someone's face was funny, especially her ugly sister's face. Pancho, though, did not think that was funny at all. He fought them all at once. Instead of punishing him, her father gave him a piece of raw steak for his eye and a shot of tequila. Here Papa culminated with a proud pat on the back.

This time, Pancho was in trouble with both the police and the gringos, although she wasn't sure why or how, just that it was *her* fault. He hadn't been around in forever, and Christi got to do whatever she wanted. Sometimes she would bring Carlos over, but if her dad found out, he would kill her, so Mona never told.

Carlos was a pimply faced guy who was actually nice to Mona and brought her

Tootsie rolls, which he knew to offer when Christi was getting herself ready. He would come in his pressed dress shirt and khaki pants. He even brought her flowers one time, but all Christi wanted to do was kiss him while Mona stayed in her room coloring. No boys were allowed in the house, not after Christi got hurt by some other boy at the quinceañera. Mona had secretly been happy someone had beat her up, until Pancho got taken away forever.

Now, Christi was on the phone in that high-pitched voice, that grated at Mona, "Hey Charlie." Mona despised how she rolled the "r" in a near-Mexican accent. She blah blah blahed, and Mona went to work.

The house was cozy, and she actually enjoyed sweeping, but she had clearly heard Mami tell Christi to sweep. Mona sighed staring at the broom. The blue wooden handle was fading from so much wear and was starting to splinter where her mother gripped it. She took the broom grudgingly and started to sweep the living room, being careful not to disturb Christi's T.V. watching and phone flirting. In no time, Mona took to the task, creating a game, going as fast as she could.

The living room was the heart of the house, and all the rooms connected to it, except for an ostracized bathroom hardly no one used. If she faced the back of the house, on the right, Pancho's room was connected to the living room with large glass doors. No one was allowed in there.

"Stupid, not in there," mumbled her sister. "Oh, not you my Carlitos!" Still, Mona looked through the glass doors. The room was dark, but she could make out the stacks of books by Asimov and other writers he would read to her. On the far wall was an enormous poster of Bruce Lee, their favorite movie star. The room looked like it always did, with his dark blue colcha with an expansive image of a lion over his bed—except that he wasn't in his room. Pancho wasn't at his desk, nose in book, reading the best parts to her.

She proceeded to the kitchen, which also connected to the living room on the right past Pancho's room. The kitchen had a square metal table and four flower-patterned chairs. It was small compared to Mrs. Rodriguez's kitchen which had a real stove. Mona's kitchen had a humble burner Papa had bought at a swap meet for $5. It rested on the sole narrow counter below the kitchen window. They did have a refrigerator an old heavy one her mother complained about because it made a constant noise, a lazy chicharra chirp of cicadas in summer. Mona wasn't allowed to open it, and Christi had threatened more than once to trap her in there, after news reports of some dumb kid accidentally hiding in a fridge just like it. The boy died during a hide-and-seek game. Mona remembered how much his mother cried on the news.

She continued to the hall, which led to the small bathroom, and she looked out the window that was a broken eye to the world. Enough sun spilled in for her to methodically collect all the dust. It was perpetually dusty in the house because they were so near the desert. When she got to the bathroom, she propped the door wide open with the trash can. She made sure to sweep around the toilet. The bathroom was small with a tiny shower only she and Pancho used. She got the metal trash bin and picked up the dust. Mona often wondered where all the dust came from and imagined tiny faeries tracking confetti into the house.

When she threw it in the small bin, Christi frightened her with a, "You missed a spot, you dummy!"

Mona swept the spot where her sister pointed, seeing nothing, and then, proceeded to sweep the room she shared with Christi. It too was linked to the living room, directly across from Pancho's room. In it, there was a large window that oversaw the dirt patio. From there, she would often see the chickens, ducks, and geese and greet them. They would always stop and greet her back. Mami and Papa's room was joined to their room with beautiful glass doors, draped with white lacy curtains her mother crafted to give them some privacy. She swept their room and found a nickel. Mona made sure to leave it on Mami's beautiful pearl colored bureau. Pancho had bought her that piece of furniture working the lettuce fields two summers in a row. Her mother wept when it was delivered, and her father complained the money could have been set aside for college.

When she finished the chore, she put the broom and dustbin away in a small closet in the kitchen. She looked at the lime green walls and immaculate counter. Christi had no food cooking on the burner. In fact, Mona knew how to cook more than her incompetent-hair-absorbed sister. She looked around, and there was nothing for her to do except clean the toilet, and even Christi wasn't cruel enough to make her do that task.

The sun still sang through the windows, and before Christi could give more phantom chores, she went outside to visit Billy and play with her duckies. Billy was a large mama goat that had surprised everyone by finally having a baby. Mona wasn't sure how babies were made, just that she had tried four times before and then, suffered a deep sadness. No one believed Mona that Billy would cry all day over her losses.

Now, she went to visit the mama first and filled up the empty water bucket with the hose. Mona continued and gave them the freshest alfalfa, digging into the pile beyond the first layer that was dried by the unmerciful sun. She breathed in the smell of fresh cut greenery and heavy goat odor. Billy Jr. took a short break from his nursing and bleated a high pitched *hellloooo* and latched back on. Mama Billy thanked her for the much-needed refreshments. Mona watered the other goats and chickens in their separate pens. They all wanted fresh alfalfa, and before the cacophony of requests annoyed her, she gave them all a bundle of freshness.

She smiled at them all and went to her favorite spot. Out in the orange groves, the borders surrounding the orchard were filled with water. Her duckie friends stopped what they were doing to come play with her. Sometimes, even new birds would perch on her head, but that would frighten her Mami, so she would ask them politely not to be around when her Mami was outside. She grabbed the first duckie, "Okay Tito, are you ready?" He shook his miniature tail and quacked. His soft yellow feathers were wonderful to touch. Often, she would rub her cheeks on them and smell their wild scent, but she wasn't sure when her sister would call her in, so she began to play.

"Hurry, hurry, hurry," Tito said.

Mona held Tito up high over the water and let him go. He dived and came back up.

"Again, again, again," it urged, but Selena was next. Mona played with the ducks for a long time, dropping one patito after the other, until the mama duck called them over. They didn't listen at first, but she admonished, "No, be good, and listen to your Mamita, always, or *La Bruja* will get you while you sleep!" The smallest one, Panchito, gave her one more pleading look before marching off with his siblings. Instantly, she regretted saying that name.

La Bruja was the only worse thing than her sister.

Mona looked between the overgrown trees. Her father was having a difficult time trimming their leaves and branches now that Pancho was gone.

Mona analyzed the sky. It was growing dark. The wind began to pick up sending sandy projectiles into her eyes. The orchard grew weirdly still, and as she stared into the darkness, she heard someone whispering her name. Perhaps it was her sister playing a trick, but her voice was never that sweet. Mona's small chest grew tight, as she peered into the heart of the orchard. It was spooky there, and she never went without her father or her mother to pick orange blossoms.

Mona said the voice. Mona knew exactly who it was. It was *La Bruja* that looked in through the window late at night or sometimes took her friends away, for good. Last week *La Bruja* had taken her father's prize fighting rooster, she was sure of it. Her mother had blamed the coyotes and made sure to have her father's rifle loaded in their locked bedroom closet.

La Bruja had started coming since last October. She had tried telling Pancho about the visits, but he told her it was just her imagination. Even at her age, Mona knew the difference between real and not real. Her dolly Kathy couldn't really talk, but her furry and feathered friends could. Even the frogs would talk to her. Her sister's hate was real. All the angry words she spat when Mami and

Papa weren't around, all the bruises were real. Mona stood there, unable to move, an erect tin soldier.

"Mona!"

She cried out. Here sister Christi was standing behind her, smirking because she had frightened her so. "Mona! I've been calling you! Get in the house. It's going to rain, little idiota."

Silky warm droplets began to fall on Mona's head, and she ran into the house and inside to the bedroom slamming the double doors behind her. She went to her coloring books, as far away from the windows as possible. Coloring always made everything better. She was working on a Cinderella picture. When she opened it, she grew sad, then angry. Her sister had colored the Bambi side next to it.

And. Signed. It.

She had used a lot of orange, filling it in perfectly, but Mona hated orange—Christi knew it.

Before she could protest, Christi walked up to Mona, pulled a few of her hairs on top of her head, turning her into a living puppet. Christi made her stand up and forced her to the kitchen. Mona squealed, as her sister manipulated her forward, but didn't dare strike back. Rubbing her head, she sat on the chair. Christi served her a tall glass of cold milk and made her a hasty peanut butter sandwich. Her special plastic pink cup was right there, on the first shelf of the cabinet.

"But it's too early! And you're s'pposed to heat the milk, Mami said. And put it in my special cup," Mona cried, "and that glass is too—"

A sharp slap snapped her face to the left.

"Don't you cry, or I'll give you another! Eat everything up," she finished with clenched teeth.

This was the sister she knew.

The pain on the side of her face was unbearable, but Mona wasn't going to give

Christi a reason to spank her, or worse, use the belt. She looked at the sloppy sandwich Christi slammed in front of her and the enormous glass of milk. Mona hated milk without chocolate, but she wasn't about to get another one.

Christi pulled a magazine from somewhere and sat next to her, making the legs of the metal chair scrape on the cheap vinyl floor. Mona cringed and glared at her sister. Christi complained, "I want a current issue, not this piece of shit that is two years old. 1977 is so old!" Mona stared at the words and the blond woman with long bangs on the cover. Her sister tried to make hers look the same, but despite her attempts, they looked curly. Even still, all her friends called her the Mexican Farrah Fawcett.

Mona couldn't read English yet, but when she did, she would never read stupid magazines. She would read the smart books like her brother read about spaceships and dragons. Christi glowered at her over the glossy cover, which compelled her to eat.

She ate her sandwich robotically with every bite sticking to her throat. The milk smelled funny and tasted lemony, but Christi never checked if it was sour or if the bread was moldy. When Pancho had watched her, he would warm her chocolate milk in the metal cup over the burner flame. Then, he would test it to make sure it was okay, occasionally adding a piece of ice. He would warm her soup, sometimes the fancy Campbell's kind from a can, but he always tasted it before he gave it to her.

Mona took a final drink. "I'm done and can't drink no more."

"Stupid, it's anymore—"

Before Christi went off on a tirade, Mona added, "I have a headache and my stomach hurts. Bad." Mona realized the headache was true and growing worse, but the stomach ache wasn't. Mona looked outside the kitchen window to the right of the table. Something dark moved against the glass. Mona sank lower in her chair. The wind began to pick up making the nasty howling sound that made her want to go pee pee.

Christi was about to hit her, again, but saw the pale complexion. Mona wasn't one to lie.

"Go to the bathroom, before you puke everywhere," snapped Christi, "and go to bed."

Mona glanced at the clock above the window. It read 7:00 p.m. because the short hand was not at her bedtime, 8:00 p.m. She knew it was way too early, and she didn't want to be in the bedroom near the window. That's where *La Bruja* came to *tap tap tap* her thin fingers against the glass. Mona tried to protest, but Christi stuck something bitter in her mouth that she swallowed with gross cold milk. Christi marched along with her to the bathroom, hovering over her until she peed, and after she was done, half dragged her to the bedroom.

She struggled to get into her pink pajamas and do the buttons and would often flip her top inside out. Pancho would encourage her, even if it took her forever. Christi just stood there with her nasty smirk. When she was done, the buttons were off, the right side longer than the left, and her sister laughed and jabbed at the air, pointing to the bed.

Mona slid under the musty covers. She stared at the last gifts Pancho had given her for Christmas—Big Bird and Cookie Monster puppets. They stood guard on the nightstand and stared at the window. She crawled out of bed and grabbed the puppets, and they all hid under the covers. When she was sad, she would press them against her face, sometimes weeping into them, when Christi was particularly awful. They never seemed to mind. Cookie Monster was the softer of the two with happy blue shiny fur. Big Bird was a rough light yolk yellow, a yarn that should have been softer, but she loved them equally.

These friends had been a total surprise.

MONA REMEMBERED THAT CHRISTMAS when there was no tree and a sad few gifts. And to beat all, the lights were out. This lack of electricity emboldened *La Bruja* to stand outside the living room window. Even without *La Bruja,* Mona had hated the dark.

She sat in the living room with her Mami. They lit candles keeping Mona safe from *La Bruja*, for a short time That night, Pancho came home late with a bag of groceries and her surprise, which she got to open early. He put on the best puppet show, although Cookie Monster called Big Bird a puto, which wasn't ever said on *Sesame Street.*

Mona smiled thinking about her brother. He had dark hair, similar to hers, and pale skin, identical to hers. He was taller than his dad and would throw his mother into a fury when he would curse.

He made up the best stories and wouldn't yell at her for playing while he studied. When Mona watched her shows, he never turned off the T.V. or read stupid magazines. He would play groovy music for her on his records and tell her about the singers. Her favorite one was about poor people that reminded her of those families living in cardboard homes along the U.S.-Mexico border. She sang bits and pieces to her friends, mixing a collage of images and off-beat notes. Then, she hummed the theme song from *Captain Kangaroo* adding some garbled English that sounded happy.

IT HAD BEEN ON A NIGHT LIKE THAT when Christi had come home from a *quinceañera*. Isabella was having a phenomenal sweet fifteen celebration, and Christi was jealous of the other girl and the glamorous party, she, could never have. Mami was asleep, and Papa was still working in the fields. Christi wasn't supposed to go out because she was only fourteen, but she lied and said she was going to the movies and then to spend the night with Lupe. She came back wearing grown-up make-up. Her disassembled mascara, making her an ugly, sad clown. She was wearing a tight pink dress, but it was torn, and she kept leaning over and crying, "Aye, Mama!"

Immediately, her Mami herded Mona back into the bedroom and told her not to come out. Then, she was ever-so afraid of what was going on in her house to pay attention to *La Bruja*. There were loud shouts, even louder when her father came home at 11:00 p.m., and they took Christi to the hospital. Mona stayed awake the whole time and was in the living room watching a late night show she didn't think was funny. Pancho would get up on occasion and look out the window, but they didn't come home until 4:00 a.m. When they got back late at night, her parents said a few words to her brother. Christi wasn't there and would be gone, to her relief, for another night. Without a word, Pancho put on his thick leather jacket, gave her a kiss on the forehead, and left.

She never saw him again.

Mami cried for weeks afterward. Once, she heard her Papa tell a close friend that he would have done the same. After that day, Christi was quiet, so quiet. For weeks, she was in their room, napping or staring out the window. As the days passed, she grew meaner. Three months later she was back to her old self.

She was jealous of Mona because Mona did what she was told, and she never begged for stuff, like Christi. Deep down in her heart, Mona knew Christi hated Mona with all her might. Hated her for no reason.

MONA DRIFTED OFF INTO SLEEP and dreamt of her animal friends and her puppets playing a game of hide and seek. In her dream, Cookie Monster could talk to her. He had a deep voice and kind eyes, not silly as the show.

It said, *Mona, don't go with her. She's not your friend.* Mona woke with a start to the *tap tap tap* at her window. It was night now, and all the crickets told their stories, sometimes in loud unison. She stared without blinking, but only saw a gnarly branch scraping the window. Sighing with relief, Mona heard her sister talking on the phone.

"I think he likes me," she giggled with exaggeration.

A long scratch made Mona sit up. She looked to the window at a pale face. Mona screamed.

"¡Chingado!" cried her sister running into the room. Pointing and shrieking, Mona stood on the bed urging her to look outside. Christi brought her down mercilessly and clamped her hand over Mona's mouth. Christi looked out the window. "There's nothing there, you idiot."

Christi raised her hand and stopped. Mona flinched anyway, but instead of the usual slap, Christi flipped her hand over and felt her forehead.

"Ah shit," she muttered. She stomped off to the bathroom medicine cabinet, where her mom kept everything from Vick's Vapor Rub to aspirin and brought back more milk.

"No! No milk," pleaded Mona. "It tastes funny."

Christi smelled and tasted the milk. "Fuck." She looked at Mona with a hint of compassion. "Does your stomach hurt?"

"Yes," whined Mona. Her stomach was cramping up like when she had chorro from eating half a watermelon. She doubled over and whimpered.

Christi cursed under her breath. "I'll make you some mint tea."

"Don't leave me," cried Mona clinging to her arm. Christi spilled some milk on the floor and shoved Mona away.

"Let go! Damnit!" She rushed off and never came back with the tea.

Mona fixed her eyes out the window. The hoot of an owl terrified her. "Cuando el tecolote canta, el indio muere," she said quietly. *When the owl sings, the Indian dies,* she explained to Cookie Monster because he didn't speak Spanish. She was part Yaqui, part Indian. It hooted staring straight at her. Then, it flew off, and the woman appeared again, smiling.

"What are you staring at?" asked her sister, holding a glass of water. She ran her hands through her bangs. "I am not cut out for this shit." Mona saw that she had taken her rollers off and fixed her hair. She wore tight jeans and a red tube top her mother did not approve of. Mona knew that meant a boy was coming over, that boy with the large eye glasses and pimpled face who brought her sweets. *Carrrrlitos!*

Christi put aspirin in Mona's mouth and made her drink the whole glass.

"Let me go into the living room with you," begged Mona. "Please! I'll be quiet."

"No! Now, shut up, or I'll lock you in!"

Mona wasn't sure if there was a lock or a key. She gave Christi one last pathetic look and hid under the covers. Without warning, Christi tore them off.

"Just use the sheet. You have a fever." With that, she left. The sheet was overly-thin, so she could make out the shapes outside.

Rain assaulted the window, as the storm raged louder. In the distance, she heard Billy and his family bleating for help. All the chickens and ducks were scared, but what terrified her was the long howl of the coyotes. They never came out when it rained, but they were out tonight, and close. She thought of her defenseless duck friends and all the baby animals.

The room grew darker, and she began to shiver.

Mona, she heard the woman whisper.

It's your imagination, she heard her brother advise. *Next time you see the witch, tell her to leave. Tell her you can't talk to strangers.*

"I can't talk to you! Go away!" she shouted.

Or if you're really scared, pray.

The scratching was louder and made her grind her teeth. *Mona, come out here.*

Mona wasn't good at praying, but she began a loud, jumbled prayer. "Jesus bless Pancho. Make *La Bruja* go away. Get me a new Barbie, brown as me. Bring Pancho home, now."

"Why are you shouting!" hollered her sister from the living room.

The voice chuckled. It was a soothing voice, but Mona knew not to trust it. Not to trust *her.*

Christi came back into the bedroom. She took one look at her sister and said, "Ah, son of a bitch. You're sweating, you loud tiny smelly pig."

She undressed Mona, getting the neckline caught on her head because she was, per-usual, carless when undoing the buttons. Christi put a thin white nightgown on her. "I'll bring you tea."

Mona begged one last time, "Let me come with you!"

Christi pushed her back into the bed. "No way, you little shit. Stop begging!" Mona tried to hang on. Christi threatened to hit her, but instead pulled three hairs from her head.

"Ouch!" Mona wanted to say more, so much more. "You meanie!"

Christi jeered, aiming her raised hand one more time, but thought better of it.

When she left, she slammed the glass doors behind her.

"What should I do Mr. Big Bird?" Mona asked her friend.

Come with us Mona, said the voice, except it was closer, near the bed. She jumped out and ran as fast as the Road Runner from Saturday morning cartoons.

Christi was watching T.V. and painting her toenails red. "What are you doing out of bed?"

Mona's mind raced. "I have to pee!"

She ran past the kitchen and then remembered the dark hall. At the end of the hall was the broken window that her father fixed with thick cardboard. She turned around, but her sister was standing behind her.

"Well, go to the bathroom and close the door like a big girl," her sister mocked

Christi knew Mona hated closing the bathroom door, day or night. She *knew* Mona was afraid of the window, and even though

Mona was sick, Christi just couldn't help herself.

Mona ran down the hall avoiding the broken window. She began closing the door and looked back.

"All the way closed," she spat as she inspected her own finger nails.

Slowly, Mona surveyed the room and checked behind the shower curtain. A lonely cockroach skittered across the immaculate floor. But it wouldn't talk to her.

Christi banged on the door. "I can't hear you pee."

She pulled down her cotton panties and sat on the cold toilet. There was only one window in the bathroom, a Mona-sized window, and she could see it clearly. There was no way *she* could get inside that window. Mona smiled for the first time that night.

She was getting comfortable being alone, when her heart stopped. The window was clouded over with something dark, the color of *La Bruja's* long tresses. Through the murky glass she saw two green eyes.

"You'd better be peeing!"

But Mona couldn't pee. She couldn't breathe. She couldn't do anything but stare at those green eyes. A loud yowl made her stand up. It was a cat, but it wasn't talking to her. It was screaming, Christi-mean insults. It said foul naughty Pancho curses at her in a Christi tone.

She whimpered and did need to pee. She sat on the toilet as a hot stream rushed out. The world began to swim, and she threw up rancid milk and peanut butter bits all over herself.

"What the hell was that!"

Christi stormed in and saw the mess. Glaring at Mona, she grabbed her, took off her gown, and put her in the shower.

"No no!" screamed Mona. "There's a mean cat outside! It wants to claw my eyes out!"

"Oh, shut up. That's just Ricky. I've been feeding him when Mom's not around." Christy turned on the water.

"It's so cold." Mona's whole body shook.

Christi grabbed the soap and lathered her up.

"It'll help cut down your fever. Fuck, of all nights they had to go to Phoenix today to that damn shit hole. Fuck! Had to take care of you." She punctuated each complaint lathering and scrubbing harder.

Christi shut the shower off and wrapped a harsh towel around her. Mona did feel better, but her Mami always said not to take a cold shower when you were sick, or else, you'd get pneumonia.

Mona muttered, "I hope I get pneumonia and die, so you'll get in trouble."

Christi stared shocked. "What the hell did you say, pendeja?"

Mona repeated over and over, "I hope I get pneumonia and die I hope I get pneumonia and die I hope I get pneumonia and die I hope I get pneumonia and die, so she won't get me. She'll get *you* instead! It's your fault he's gone! You're the *pendeja*, you *pinch*e slut." Mona spat anger, and Christi was at a loss for words.

Christi picked her up gently and carried her to bed, as Mona ranted out a litany of foulness.

IN THE DISTANCE, Christi called a neighbor on the phone.

"I don't know what to do. She's really sick. What? Roasted aloe? Are you sure?"

Mona shivered under the sheet and could not stop. She took Big Bird and Cookie Monster and kicked them out.

"You jerks. Why did you let Pancho leave? Fuckers!"

She looked out the window. There *she* was again. Mona could see her full, luminescent body. Mona tried to look away and focus on the distant fruit, but her eyes were being stubborn. Mona wondered what colors she would use to fill that whiteness. *La Bruja* was beautiful with long black hair that reached her ankles, except this time she was naked. Mona had only seen her mom without clothes, but she didn't look as curvy and graceful as *La Bruja*. Everything about the woman was shimmery. Through feverish eyes, Mona saw the owl perched on her left shoulder. He wasn't mean like the cat.

"What's his name?" she asked.

Muerte, answered the woman in echoes. Mona asked shyly, if the woman was going to kill her, but she said there was no way. *La Bruja* explained that Mona was precious to her, more precious than she was to her own Mami.

"Why won't you leave me alone?" asked Mona.

Mona, come with us. Monaaaaa.

Christi marched in. "Who are you talking to?"

"Pancho said not to talk to strangers. But I've seen her for so long, and Muerte seems nice."

Christi gave a fearful glance out the window. "There's no one there. Lie back."

Mona did as she was told—obedient Mona—until her sister placed something hot on the soles of her feet.

"Stay still," cried the witch, "this will bring your fever down."

"It burns!" Mona felt the searing heat on her other foot. "Why are you hurting me? It hurts! You said I was precious. You're a big fat mentirosa, just like Christi!"

Christi became *La Bruja,* became Christi. Both began to tear up. "It'll make you better. Mrs. Rodriguez said so."

Mona began to cry in earnest. When the roasted aloe had cooled, Christi took the limp green plant off.

"Ah shit!" she said. "Damn, it was too hot. Mona, I'll get some toothpaste for the burns. They're tiny, as teeny tiny as your brain, so don't worry, okay?" Christi stared uncertain of what to do. It didn't matter, Mona passed out.

IN A FITFUL SLEEP, THE CAT SCRATCHED at the soles of her feet. The woman was smiling at her, holding a cold cherry ice pop, just outside the window. Enticing her to go into the night. She awoke with a start to the sound of her sister on the phone. Christi was crying to someone.

"Mami! Mona is really sick—"

Mona felt a large boulder in her stomach. She stepped on the floor. It hurt bad, but she really needed to go. If she walked on her toes like Billy, the pain lessened. She tiptoed past her sister who was preoccupied on the sofa and went into the kitchen. She slowed at the long dark hallway. Only the living room light was on, and it wasn't enough. Mona turned to find Christi, but as she walked back to the living room, she heard Pancho.

It's okay I'm over here. I'm behind the bathroom door.

It *was* Pancho! He never put roasted aloe on her feet or gave her yucky milk. Pancho had come home at last! She moved as fast as she could and looked to the reinforced window. The cardboard was missing.

Mona stopped. A cold chill ran in through the hole. She looked to the tree outside, and something black emerged. Right there was the ugly dark Ricky who was somehow larger and filling up the entire gaping hole. It yowled at her, and she screamed. She walked backwards and ran into something. Mona turned, hoping to see her Pancho; her face went that tantrummy green. It was *her,* with her pale flesh.

In the darkness, she was white, gringa white, as American soap opera heroines. With endless hair and dark eyes that seeped into her face. Mona tried to run toward the bathroom, but she held her in strong arms, fixed as the roots of trees older than Pancho. The woman genuflected and sat terrified Mona on her knee. She smelled of pond water and new tadpoles, of orchard wildness Mona loved. The witch took Mona's feet and caressed them lovingly. The pain went away, and the woman smiled wide.

Her crooked teeth were black, the color of old dog shit. A foul stench came out of her mouth. Mona stared in awe as an earthworm crawled out of her right ear, but when the coral snake crawled out of the woman's putrid mouth, she screamed and wet herself, a long gush running down the *La Bruja's* legs. She laughed, not a witchy laugh like cartoons, something soft and more dangerous.

CHRISTI RAN INTO THE HALLWAY. "Mona!" She slipped and fell hard on her tailbone. She grew furious when she smelled urine and called louder, "MONA! YOU JUST FUCKING WAIT!"

She stood up cursing all the while and went into the bathroom. "Where are you, you stupid bitch?"

Turning on the light, she searched everywhere, but Mona wasn't there. She went back out into the hallway and saw the wind had knocked the cardboard down.

"Mona?" In the hole was a disgusting black matted cat. A slow hiss made her take a step back. "That's not Ricky. Ricky's a white cat." The blood began to pound in her head, giving her a piercing headache that radiated down to her spine. Christi searched the shower. She looked in the bathroom three times.

She's outside she thought. Christi remembered Mona say she wanted to see her friends.

And what had Pancho said about

Mona? *She's special. She can see things no one else can.* Perfect special Mona.

The bitch was going to get it.

Christi searched in the kitchen cupboards and went through every room, turning on the lights as she went. Finally, she searched the bedroom. A lump on the bed gave her a sigh of relief. The covers were back on neatly. She turned on the lights and overturned the heavy blanket. She yelped. It was a large piece of wood the length of Mona's body and a wet burlap sack. Something moved inside. The tree branch was slimy and skeletal. Christi shivered. "Damn it Mona." But she knew deep down, Mona hadn't done that. Breathing in spasms, she opened the sack expecting the worst. Out came three dead kittens, newborns, and a white one that was still alive. Christi began to cry. "What the fuck is going on?"

She took the kitten to her chest. "Poor baby. Freezing cold." Disgusted, she grabbed the other ones and put them back in the sack with the tippy tip of her fingers. She looked one last time outside the window. The next curse died in her throat. There *were* fingerprints and scratch marks. Real ones.

"No no no!" Christi turned to get the phone and screamed.

"¡Que susto!" said Mrs. Rodriguez putting her hands to her chest, "I walked over as soon as it stopped raining. I'm sorry I startled you, but the door was wide open. Your mama called me. They won't be back until tomorrow. Said the dust storm was too bad and with this rain, forget it. They say your brother is okay, though." She looked around concerned, "Where is Monita?"

"She took her! Mona tried to tell me, but I wouldn't listen. You have to help me find her."

Christi ran outside and looked in all the places Mona might play, but it was too dark. A few minutes later Mrs. Rodriguez called out, "Come back in! You'll catch a cold, mija."

Christi walked in shivering.

Mrs. Rodriguez put her shawl over the girl's shoulders. "I'll go look with a flashlight. Where's your dad's flashlight?"

AN HOUR LATER, Mr. Rodriguez came back without Mona. Against her better judgment, Mrs. Rodriguez called the police. She knew dear Mona was not one to run away or pull pranks. She was a clever girl, not reckless.

When the police came, Christi was still clutching the kitten to her chest. It slept, warm against her breasts.

A young police officer checked her out and asked, *Is there any reason she might have run away? Did you get into a fight? Why was the front door unlocked?*

Christi chuckled. *She took her. She took her. It didn't matter if it was locked or not.*

The police looked outside the window and looked at the strange piece of wood. One of them even looked at the sack full of dead kittens. *These yours?*

She answered coldly, *No. Never seen them before.* When the police left, Mrs. Rodriguez pried the kitten from her hands and fed it some milk.

"What a cutie, all white. Go to sleep. I'm sure she'll be back in the morning. Maybe the storm scared her." The kind neighbor found an old cleaning rag in the broom closet, an old white t-shirt and tore it into strips. She made a nest and put it on Christi's chest, where the kitten cuddled. It gave a wide yawn and fell asleep within seconds.

THE SUN BURST THROUGH THE WINDOWS, ERASING the darkness from the previous night. Christi woke up on the sofa. Her back was uncomfortable. She called out for Mona, but no one answered. A small bundle of rags lay over her chest. She got up and looked around. No one was in the house. She sighed and looked where she had lain. It was quiet at last, and she ran her fingers through her bangs. She would trim them again.

She remembered the previous night and recalled the white fur ball. She ran her hands to what was poking her and sat up. She let out a small cry, then forced herself to stop before she started to cry in earnest. Sometime in her sleep, she had crushed the kitten to death. She swallowed a thick lump and picked the corpse up. It was cold and flattened, with its tiny tongue sticking out to the right. Christi took it and held it to her chest and despite hurting her manicure, went out to bury it in the patio where Mona liked to play.

TWO WEEKS LATER, Christi still refused to cry. In those weeks, a series of awfulness befell the house. Not only was Pancho going to an adult prison, but Mona was nowhere to be found. Her dad nearly lost his job because he spent so much time looking for her, a drunken loco in the groves. What really got her emotional was the death of the kitten. She wiped at her eyes, worried her make-up would smear. Christi walked into the house. She sat on the couch and extended her whole body.

The days after Mona was kidnapped, her mother walked around like a ghost, and barely spoke to anyone, but this time she came out of the kitchen and said, "Did you feed the chickens?"

"Come on," she said on reflex, "I'm busy. Have Mona do it!"

The look Mama gave her chilled Christi to the core, and without arguing anymore, she went outside. It was 5:30 p.m. and most of the stupid chickens were in the pen. They clucked at her expectantly, some trying to peck her feet. She kicked at them.

"Stay the fuck off my polish!" The wind began to pick up, as she grabbed a metal bowl and filled it with feed.

The earthy smell of cracked wheat turned her stomach. She overfilled the bowl and put some in the coup's feeding trough.

"Peet, peet, peet," she said trying to usher all the chickens in. She hated feeding the chickens but despised putting them in the pen. Mona normally did that job, and the retarded chickens did what she told them.

She thought, *Stupid Mona.*

A straggling black chicken with most of the feathers missing from her head pecked at her hard. Christi kicked and kicked.

"Stop being so mean to my friends!" the voice said right behind her.

Christi jumped and screamed. She turned around. "Mona!" The ethereal command repeated over and over retreating to the orchard. She ran toward the voice tripping and getting scratched up by the orange branches that were not trimmed. She fell slamming her mouth on the muddy ground.

She called again, but Mona was not there. She got on her knees and stood up, her knees trembling.

"I'm sorry!" she cried with all her might. "I'm sorry Mona! Please come back! Mama, your Mami, needs you!" Choking a sob, she breathed in. "I need you!"

A delicate blue butterfly flew in front of her eyes and landed on her nose. The orchard grew still and warm like a hug, but Mona was nowhere.

When she stood up an enormous owl perched on a low jutting branch and stared at her, silent. It had no business being out so early.

"Fuck off," she said, and stormed back toward the house. When she got to the spot where she had buried the kitten, Christi gasped. Mona was crouched on the ground staring at the dirt. She was not quite there but a smoky illusion, fading in and out.

Mona turned to look at her and smiled. "She's not so bad, *La Bruja*. She doesn't hit me, like you. Never yells or makes me feel small." Mona looked into her eyes. Christi saw her pudgy cherubic face, sometimes clear, sometimes hazy. Her little sister smiled benevolently, but her eyes no longer sparkled.

"Mona!" Christi ran to her to scoop her up, but her sister vanished like a dust devil in summer.

She clutched at the dirt and shouted her name over and over bringing her mother out. "Mama!" said Christi pulling at her own hair. "She was just here!"

Christi begged and pleaded for Mona to return, "I promise I'll be nice! I swear on my life. MONA!"

Her mother reached for her and held her, firm. They both sobbed into each other. When she stopped, she heard a familiar sound. Behind a mint plant, she heard the mewling of the kitten.

"What?" asked Christi. It was alive with the same playful clumsiness from weeks ago. Mona had brought it to life somehow. She turned to look for her again among the trees, but even the owl was gone.

When she returned to the dirt patio, her mother was sitting on an upside-down plastic bucket. Holding the white kitten, she said, "Mona would have loved it."

"Mom," she knelt next to her Mama, "I know it sounds crazy, but she was here. And, and, I think if I am good for her, she'll come back, Mama." Christi babbled on, spilling every terrible cruelty she could remember doing to her sister. Especially the time she made her eat a cricket.

Her mother sighed. "I hope so Christi. I hope she comes back."

Christi looked to the sky and thought long and hard. Sweat ran down her face, and the scratches were beginning to sting from the salt. She ignored all that pain and the humiliation of looking like she had been dragged through the street just as she had so many weeks ago when that boy had been so awful to her. Christi cringed as the familiar rage radiated through her, that rage she didn't know how to quit.

SHE HAD BEEN DANCING with him, that tall curly-haired boy who always wore jeans and white t-shirts at parties. She had seen him a couple of times, and when he asked her out to dance, and all the girls turned to her with envy, she had practically jumped at the chance.

He was nineteen, still had not graduated, but she did not care. After a couple of slow dances, he had taken her outside into the parking lot, when the music picked up, promising to show her something cool. The "cool thing" was a regular brown Buick, not fancy, but it was a car that could take her to new destinations, even L.A. It was parked further away from all the cars under a mesquite tree. He opened the door, and she sat eagerly. She settled, the hot seat sticking to her legs. "Ring My Bell" blared from the radio, and she asked him to change the station, but he turned it up louder instead.

Christi had been excited to have her first real kiss, but before she could part her lips, he had slammed her face onto the polished dashboard. She tried to scream, but he clamped his hand over her perfect mouth.

"I'll fucking cut you if you make a noise. Ruin that pretty face!" She had not doubt he carried a knife.

Her legs grew weak, and she tried to vanish somewhere else, but he kept cursing at her and biting her. He ripped at her dress and shredded her new purple lace underwear in one go. He was almost twice her size, and he pinned her down, suffocating her, while he gripped her mouth shut with his enormous hand. Her teeth were starting to bite her own mouth on the inside from the force, and she began to cry when the warmth and wetness spread between her legs.

Her ran her index finger down below, gently, just as she had imagined it would be, and she tried not to moan. He licked her face and whispered in her ear, "You like that you dirty slut? You want me, don't you, you puta?"

He released her mouth and clamped onto her, biting her tongue. She remembered he tasted of cigarettes and onions and wanted to puke.

The heat and pain that followed was unbearable. His penis was rough like sandpaper and unyielding, stabbing her repeatedly. Though it didn't last long, she felt like she had been ripped apart for hours. But the most humiliating part wasn't that he had thrown her to the side of the car and driven away. That a lot of people had seen her with her messed up dress and running mascara. Her hair a wreck. It wasn't the humiliation of one of her dad's friends giving her an endless ride home. No. The worst part was that he had stepped outside as she crawled away and urinated all over her, even her head.

Minutes later, she hated herself and her erratic amnesia. She could not remember his name or his face because he didn't go to her high school. She was sure that was why, yet she just recalled his damned creased Levi jeans and immaculate white shirt with her blood on it like dots on a map. The family friend who drove her home did know who he was, and told her father straight away, went as far as to offer to go after him. Unfortunately, so did Pancho. Her older brother knew exactly who he was and went off in his bad leather jacket with a bat and a hammer, driving off in his blue pick-up truck.

It was heroic.

According to the police, Pancho made him pay ten times over for what he did to her, but it wasn't enough. Not for Christi.

SHE STILLED HERSELF. Looking at her mom into her empty, tired eyes, she swore an oath to God and the Virgencita María. Christi held her mother's hand while she did it. She would become the daughter her parents needed. She would be the sister Mona had wanted.

Her mother tensed for a moment and steeled her hand. Mama stared off into the distance and did not say a word. It would take more than promises to convince her, but for now, she had her one daughter left who needed the most help of all. Her stupid cruel daughter whom she loved with all her might. Maybe Mona would return some day.

"Mona, please come home," her mother began, and both finished together, almost a prayer. They repeated it over and over putting all their souls into the litany. They waited for a time, as the new kitten played with Mami's braid. Christi scrutinized it, but it purred and seemed normal. Mami looked all around the orchard and the patio one last time.

When nothing happened, they walked into their home to prepare supper. Her father would be tired.

"Today, I'm going to show you how to cut the tomatoes and onions," Mami said and to her surprise, when they were in the kitchen, Christi put on an apron and took out the knife from the kitchen drawer.

"I swear, I'll be good," Christi muttered.

Her mother's face tightened, as she remembered her lost children. Still, Mami kissed her forehead and patiently showed her the steps.

The End

La Inspiración

This inspiration is dedicated to the children of Gaza, Ukraine, Haiti, and asylum seekers in the United States.

Where do *your* horror stories scream from? Books? Movies? Folklore? Childhood trauma?

For me, it is all of those and more. As a person of color, horror comes from the history of colonialism, racism, sexism, and exploitation. That is *real* horror that you can only run from and heal by reading. Maybe writing work like this one.

As a child, I would escape into all manner of stories, including Revelations which I read in the second grade, something I recommend to no one. It terrified me, the thought of the end of the world, visions of fire and blood became alive so alive I had nightmares for weeks. Add on top of that the airing of *The Day After* which I saw on November 20, 1983, on A.B.C., during a time when Gorbachev and Reagan were slinging rocks at each other like angry niños in the barrio. I was eleven at the time and just beginning to understand world politics. The possibility of nuclear war was constantly in the backdrop.

Then came the what ifs.

We all have them.

What if I wasn't good enough to enter Heaven? What about el Chamuco, the Devil, Mami would tell me would take me away if I didn't listen? Then, there were the cuentos about La Bruja.

Stories of La Bruja were a steady staple, cautionary tales: *Be good and listen to Mama or else, La Bruja will get you*! This was not the only tool in the parental arsenal meant to keep us kids docile and in check, but it was the one they would drill into us.

Despite my parents' intentions, La Bruja fascinated me, this woman with unlimited power to take children and teach them a lesson. Where did she come from? Why did God allow her such strength? Was she eating the naughtiest children? By all accounts, she was independent and a force to be reckoned with, even by adults.

In the telling of her tales, none of these questions were answered, and they were not meant to be, because it was the not knowing that sent children straight to bed and cowering under blankets.

Then, there was the known: my older sister. In this novelette, I modeled a lot of the brutal beatings, based on what my sister did to me. Now, to be fair, my sister and I have buried the hatchet about these happenings, recently in fact. She apologized and meant it. Even without that, I have learned to love her dearly. She is one of my strongest supporters but back then was a different matter. That fear of getting "it" was palpable. There wasn't a day I didn't have to walk on eggshells or hide from her, often running behind my large abuelita, my grandmother and best friend, to shield me.

At the same time, I was no angel. I wished awful things to happen to my older sister and thank goodness they never did. I mean, I think most kids wish evil upon their siblings, but I carried that grudge for a long time! Decades.

I would relive some of the worst days. It took me decades to be able to write this story, yet I managed to capture much of the resentment I held into the work and capture the abject horror of living with a bully, a meat and bone nightmare that never quit.

And that, dear reader, is the legit origin of *La Bruja in the Orchard*! It was cathartic to write. It was an intense joy to delve into this folktale and make it my own. I loved the complexity of *this* bruja, so much that I plan to expand this universe into a novel.

I hope you enjoyed this short tale! I hope it scared you, maybe to the point of snuggling under a colcha. Mostly, I pray it will inspire you, perhaps, to heal because the world can be brutal, especially for children from the barrios of the world.

Acknowledgements: ¡Muchas Gracias, Todos!

Un gran abrazo y beso to my amazing husband Aaron, my supportive children Antonio and Simona. I need to thank my little sister, Diana who reads all my work, and Laura Garcia and Adam Gottlieb for their encouragement and continued kind words. A special gratitude to my good friend Eric Allen Yankee for his guru advice. Thank you all who have been reading my drafts, especially Jerome Cusson and Ximena Escobar for the thoughtful feedback on this story. Support team, you all know who you are, and there are not enough words to express my appreciation. Monique Landsberger deserves a huge gratitude for her editing and copy-editing expertise. I have not forgotten you readers—muchísimas gracias for supporting my creations. Finally, a special thank you to my 'Ama and 'Apa, whose sacrifices made this amazing writing life possible.

About the Author

MARIA J. ESTRADA is an English college professor of Composition, Literature, and her favorite, Creative Writing. She grew up in the desert outside of Yuma, Arizona in the real *Barrio de Los Locos*, a barrio comprised of new Mexican immigrants and first-generation Chicanos. Drawing from this setting and experiences, she writes like a *loca* every minute she can—all while magically balancing her work and family obligations. She lives in Chicago's south side with her wonderful husband, two remarkable children, and two mischievous cats. You can learn more about her other books and writing happenings at barrioblues.com.

BOOKS BY MARIA J. ESTRADA

ZOMBIES IN THE BARRIO SERIES

The Long Walk

LA BRUJA DEL BARRIO LOCO WORLD

La Bruja in the Orchard
La Bruja del Barrio Loco
Mona's Return
A Not So Magical Day

Wolf Trek

Zona 5

Not Your Abuelita's Folktales

One Last Favor. . .

If you enjoyed this or any other works by me, follow me, Dr. Maria J. Estrada on Amazon or Goodreads (goodreads.com/DrMariaJEstrada)!

You can also drop me a short review on Amazon and Goodreads.

Thank you, Readers! I am honored by your support.

-M. Estrada

www.ingramcontent.com/pod-product-compliance
Lightning Source LLC
Chambersburg PA
CBHW030336310726
48979CB00001B/62

* 9 7 8 1 9 5 4 4 4 4 0 7 2 *